Gearhead Garage

DIRT BIKES

DEANNA CASWELL

WORLD BOOK

This World Book edition of *Dirt Bikes*
is published by agreement between
Black Rabbit Books and World Book, Inc.
© 2018 Black Rabbit Books,
2140 Howard Dr. West,
North Mankato, MN 56003 U.S.A.
World Book, Inc.,
180 North LaSalle St., Suite 900,
Chicago, IL 60601 U.S.A.

Jennifer Besel, editor; Grant Gould, interior designer; Michael Sellner,
cover designer; Omay Ayres, photo researcher

Library of Congress Control Number: 2016049998

ISBN: 978-0-7166-9303-1

Printed in the United States at CG Book Printers,
North Mankato, Minnesota, 56003. 3/17

CONTENTS

CHAPTER 1

Fast

and Loud

The dirt bike whizzes down the track. A tail of dirt sprays behind it. The bike starts up a ramp. The driver twists the **throttle** and zooms into the air. The bike hangs for a second. Then it lands with a thud. With no time to pause, the rider speeds to the finish line.

What Is a Dirt Bike?

Dirt bikes are off-road motorcycles. They aren't meant for street riding. They are made for twists, turns, and jumps.

Dirt bikes have tough **frames**. Bumps and hard landings won't break them. Their knobby tires grip mud and sand. These bikes are great for racing or off-road riding.

DIRT BIKE PARTS

THROTTLE

EXHAUST PIPES

FENDER

FRAME

ENGINE

FOOT PEG

TIRES

Heights of Enduro Bikes

KTM 250 XC-F

Yamaha WR250F

Husqvarna TE 250

BETA 250 RR-Race-2-Stroke

height at seat   34

Racing Bikes

Enduro bikes are one type of racing dirt bike. These bikes are used for long-distance races. Enduro races last days. Enduro bikes have large **fuel** tanks.

Motocross bikes race on closed tracks. These bikes are light and very tough. Riders use them to make huge jumps.

39.06 inches (99 centimeters)

38 inches (97 cm)

37.8 inches (96 cm)

36.6 inches (93 cm)

35   36   37   38   39   40

2015 BETA 250 RR-Race
2-Stroke enduro bike

PRICE
$8,799

WEIGHT
229 **pounds**
(104 kilograms)

2016 Yamaha YZ250F
motocross bike

PRICE
$7,590

WEIGHT
231 **pounds**
(105 kilograms)

2015 Suzuki DR-Z400S dual-sport bike

PRICE
$6,599

WEIGHT
317 pounds
(144 kilograms)

2016 Honda CRF250X trail bike

PRICE
$8,440

WEIGHT
269 pounds
(122 kilograms)

Other Kinds of Dirt Bikes

Trail bikes are for off-road fun. They are more comfortable than racing bikes. Trail bikes are not for high speeds. But they are great for riding in the woods.

Dual-sport bikes work for on- and off-road travel. Drivers can use them on city streets. They have lights and rearview mirrors. The tires work well on roads and trails.

CHAPTER 2

The History of Dirt Bikes

Motorcycle racing became popular in the early 1900s. Riders in England and the United States developed race courses. Riders weaved around rocks and streams. But the motorcycles weren't built for racing in dirt. Their tires spun out. They scraped over rocks. Their electrical systems wouldn't work when they got wet.

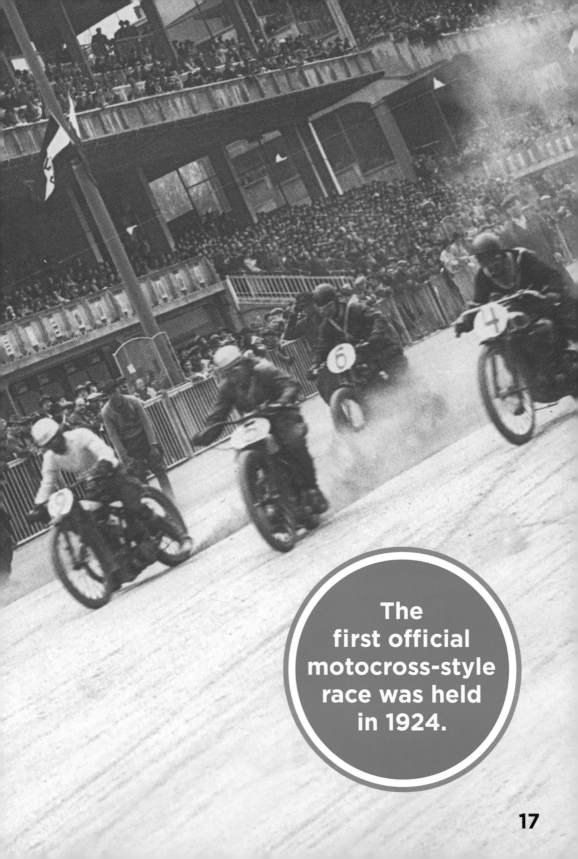

The
first official
motocross-style
race was held
in 1924.

Getting Faster

Technology continued to improve dirt bikes. Plastic was developed in the 1930s. Then in the 1950s, a scientist made big changes to the two-stroke engine. He made the engine simple and powerful.

People began using plastic parts and the new engine on bikes. Plastic pieces made bikes lighter. The new engine made bikes fast and fun.

The changes the scientist made to the engine are still used today.

By the Numbers

Dirt bikes today are fast machines.

$1,399 to $8,440

COST OF
TRAIL BIKES
IN 2016

ABOUT
500,678

NUMBER OF MOTORCYCLES
SOLD IN THE UNITED STATES
IN 2015

ABOUT

73 MILES

(118 KILOMETERS) PER GALLON

BEST FUEL USAGE

of a 2016 Honda CRF250L
dual-sport bike

200
POUNDS
(91 KG)

AVERAGE
WEIGHT
OF A DIRT BIKE

125 MILES
(201 km) per hour

TOP SPEED OF A
2015 BMW R 1200 GS ADVENTURE

CHAPTER 3

TunedUp

Riders control their bikes with their hands and feet. The right handle is the throttle. It's like a gas pedal. The **clutch** is on the left handle. The clutch releases the **gears**. Drivers change gears with their left feet to go faster or slower. They use their right feet to press the rear brake.

Bike Control

handlebars

clutch

brake

Shocks and Chunky Treads

Dirt bikes are used for bumpy rides. But landing big jumps can be painful for riders. Shocks absorb the force of bumps. Riders can do amazing tricks.

Most dirt bikes have knobby tires.

Deep **treads** grab onto thick mud and rocks.

The tires don't spin out on
wet or sandy trails.

CHAPTER 4

The Future of Dirt Bikes

Technology will continue to improve dirt bikes. The newest advancement is air shocks. Honda put them on dirt bikes in 2013. They work better on hard landings. Riders can adjust them easily with a pump.

Maybe computers or 3-D printing will change future bikes. But one thing will stay the same. Dirt bikes will always be fast and fun.

1950s

People begin using plastic parts and a new engine.

1924

Drivers hold the first motocross-style race.

1885

First motorcycle is invented.

1885

World War II ends.

1945

The first people walk on the moon.

1969

1975

Yamaha releases Monoshocks.

2013

Air shocks become standard on Hondas.

2016

The Mount St. Helens volcano erupts.

1980

Terrorists attack the World Trade Center and Pentagon.

2001

clutch (KLUTCH)—a part used to connect and disconnect pieces that drive a machine

enduro (in-DUR-oh)—a long race

exhaust (ig-ZOST)—the mixture of gases produced when an engine burns fuel

frame (FRAYM)—the structure that supports the body of a motorcycle or automobile

fuel (FEYUL)—a material, such as coal, oil, or gas, that is burned to produce heat or power

gear (GEER)—a part that connects the engine of a vehicle to the wheels and controls the speed at which the wheels turn

throttle (THRAH-tuhl)—a device that controls the flow of fuel to an engine

tread (TREHD)—the pattern of raised lines on the surface of a tire

BOOKS

Brooklyn, Billie B. *Motorcycle Racing.* Checkered Flag. New York: PowerKids Press, 2015.

Ciovacco, Justine. *Motorcycles.* Let's Find Out! Transportation. New York: Britannica Educational Publishing in association with Rosen Educational Services, 2017.

Scheff, Matt. *Dirt Bikes.* Speed Machines. Minneapolis: Abdo Publishing, 2015.

WEBSITES

Dirt Bikes and Off-Road News
www.motorcycle-usa.com/dirt-bike

Freestyle Motocross
www.freestyle-motocross.net

Motocross
www.kidzworld.com/article/6121-motocross-101

INDEX